1952 CHEVY STYLELINE DELUXE

1952 BUICK SPECIAL

1956 FORD FAIRLANE
CROWN VICTORIA

1959 CADILLAC
SERIES 62

"Cara Cara"

1954 CHEVY 210 SERIES

1959 DeSOTO
FIREDOME

1958 EDSEL
CITATION

1950 OLDSMOBILE
ROCKET 88

1959 FORD THUNDERBIRD

55 BUICK ROADMASTER

1957 FORD COUNTRY SEDAN STATION WAGON

1957 CHEVY
BEL AIR

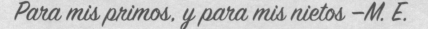

Para mis primos, y para mis nietos —M. E.

Para Erick, mi hermano viajero —M. C.

I thank God for people who keep working to solve overwhelming problems instead of giving up. I'm grateful for the inspiring ingenuity and perseverance of the Cuban people in the face of more than half a century of poverty and scarcity. Special thanks to Laura Godwin for the fantastic idea, Mike Curato for his stunning illustrations, my cousins for showing him around the island, my wonderful agent, Michelle Humphrey, and the entire publishing team. —*M. E.*

Henry Holt and Company, *Publishers since 1866*
175 Fifth Avenue, New York, New York 10010
mackids.com

Henry Holt® is a registered trademark of Macmillan Publishing Group, LLC.
Text copyright © 2017 by Margarita Engle
Illustrations copyright © 2017 by Mike Curato
All rights reserved.

Library of Congress Cataloging-in-Publication Data is available.
ISBN 978-1-62779-642-2

Our books may be purchased in bulk for promotional, educational, or business use.
Please contact your local bookseller or the Macmillan Corporate and Premium Sales Department at (800) 221-7945 ext. 5442 or by e-mail at MacmillanSpecialMarkets@macmillan.com.

First edition—2017 / Designed by April Ward
The artist used pencil acrylic, paper, photo overlay, digital color in Adobe Photoshop, and other mixed media to create the illustrations for this book.
Printed in China by RR Donnelley Asia Printing Solutions, Ltd., Dongguan City, Guangdong Province

10 9 8 7 6 5 4 3 2 1

Margarita Engle

ALL THE WAY TO

Havana

illustrated by *Mike Curato*

GODWIN BOOKS

Henry Holt and Company · New York

We have a gift, and we have a cake,
and today we're going to drive all the way
to the big city to see my new baby cousin
on his zero-year birthday!

Some of this island's old cars purr like kittens,
but ours is so tired that she just chatters
like a busy chicken—

cara cara, cara cara,
cluck, cluck, cluck...

Today Cara Cara sounds like a tiny baby chick.

Pío pío,
pío pío,
pffffft.

Papá opens the trunk and lets me hand him
the heavy toolbox. Then he raises the hood
to show me all the rattling parts
that have been fixed with wire, tape,
and mixed-up scraps of dented metal.

He listens to each tapping *taca taca* noise
that Cara Cara makes as together we struggle
to fix all the grunts, squeals, and grumbling

clunk clunks
that should be busy
cluck, cluck,
clucks.

I choose a wrench, and a bolt, and a belt. . . .

No luck, but we keep trying and trying,
even though all the silly noises
are still a mystery
unsolved.

We don't give up.
We experiment.
We invent!

A twist here.
A tightening there.
Move this.
Hold that.

Try one way,
then the other . . .

until finally, after discouraging minutes that feel like endless hours, Cara Cara once again begins to sound like a chattering hen!

CUBA C090815

The road is bumpy, and our noisy car ends up
so crowded with friendly neighbors who need a ride
that I feel like we're traveling in a barrel of elbows and knees.

But we have a gift, and we have a cake,
and we're driving to my new baby cousin's
zero-year birthday!

and we
zoom zoom—

zoom

cluck
cluck
cluck

beside farms, forests, beaches, and forts,

toward the curved road by the seawall,
where Mamá points out noisy old cars of every color—
yellow, pink, purple, green, orange,
and even a bright red car
with huge fins
like a lurking
shark.

I'm glad that Cara Cara is peacefully blue, like the clear sky above and the wide sea beyond.

Some of the noisy old cars around us
have torn seats, shattered windows,
and cracked mirrors.

Many of the cars
roar, growl, whine,
or ***putt putt,***

but most just **honk, honk, honk**

as they glide

bumpety
bump

on potholed city streets,

where people lean
over crumbling balconies
as laundry dances
and a sea breeze

sings.

When we finally reach Tía's house,
I hug Abuelo, and everyone smiles
as we admire the funny baby boy
who is too little to know how to open a gift,

or play with the box and the ribbon, or
build a teetering mango and pineapple tower!

After lunch, cake, music, and a happy birthday fiesta, I need a quiet siesta. But when I wake up, I discover that it's already time to start driving home.

So we zoom and bump all the way back
to our little village, where we will soon
have a chance to

cara cara
taka taka
pío pío
clunk

sleep.

The next morning, we have to work under the hood
once again, never giving up, never losing hope. . . .
I'm eager to help Papá guess
which tool is best.

When he asks me which city-trip car I liked most,
the answer is easy—our car! This noisy blue one,
with its ragged seats and cloudy windows,
because Cara Cara already belonged to our family
on the day when Abuelo, my old grandpa,
celebrated *his* zero-year
birthday.

Someday Abuelo's car will be yours, Papá promises,
making me feel as proud and powerful
as the bold eagle that makes Cara Cara's
sky-blue hood
look so brave!

Author's Note

*D*ue to a complex historical situation, many of the American cars on the island of Cuba are pre-1959 and so old that parts under the hood have been replaced many times, often with makeshift inventions. Despite more than half a century of poverty and hardship, the Cuban people remain so creative that they manage to keep machines of all sorts running long past the age when wealthier people would discard them. This simple poem about the island's noisy old cars is intended as an expression of admiration for the everyday ingenuity of poor people everywhere who have to struggle, persevere, create, and invent on a daily basis, never losing hope. Undoubtedly, a boy like the one in this story would dream of modern cars and space-age inventions along with plans to keep his family's antique car running smoothly.

Illustrator's Note

I had the great fortune to visit Cuba to research this book. My friend and fellow artist Erick Ledesma came with me to act as a translator. We stayed with Margarita's cousins, Julio and Isabel, at their *casa particular* (the Cuban equivalent of a bed-and-breakfast) in the heart of Havana. We hired a driver named Rey, who picked us up in a 1954 Chevy 210 Series (also known as the Chevy Delray—no pun intended). The car has been in his wife Marbelis's family for more than thirty years. Rey and Marbelis drove Erick and me across the beautiful Cuban countryside and back to Havana. I wanted to experience the trip that the family in this book makes.

I created the illustrations by combining pencil drawings, paintings, and textures from photographs I took while in Cuba. Some auto experts might look at this book and point out "mistakes" in the cars I drew. In Cuba, people have to work with what they have, so some cars have parts that used to belong to completely different cars (and sometimes entirely different machines!). This includes Cara Cara, who has a different steering wheel, rearview mirror, side mirrors, reflective orange decals where the front white blinkers used to be, and a completely different engine. She's also missing a few chrome details here and there, but she still looks good and gets people where they need to go.

Rey and Marbelis now call their '54 Chevy "Cara Cara," so she *is* real. For me, she has come to represent everything that I love about Cuba: classic beauty, perseverance, and family loyalty.

1958 CHEVY IMPALA

1956 FORD THUNDERBIRD

1956 PLYMOUTH FURY

1957 DODGE
CORONET

1953 PONTIAC CHIEFTAIN

1958 LINCOLN
CONTINENTAL

1950 CHEVY
3100 PICKUP

1954 FORD
CRESTLINE VICTORIA

1960 BUICK
ELECTRA

1956 MERCURY
MONTCLAIR

1940 CHEVY MASTER DELUXE

1953 CADILLAC SERIES 62